For Ethan, Evan, Everett, Asher, Emery, and Bailey.
With Love.

— K. L. W.

For those who leave family and country behind
to pursue a better life, regardless of fear.

— S. P.

Text © 2021 Karen Lynn Williams • Illustrations © 2021 Sara Palacios

Published in 2021 by Eerdmans Books for Young Readers, an imprint of Wm. B. Eerdmans Publishing Co. • Grand Rapids, Michigan

www.eerdmans.com/youngreaders • All rights reserved • Manufactured in China

29 28 27 26 25 24 23 22 21   1 2 3 4 5 6 7 8 9

ISBN 978-0-8028-5490-2 • A catalog record of this book is available from the Library of Congress

Illustrations created with digital materials

Facing Fear

AN IMMIGRATION STORY

WRITTEN BY
KAREN LYNN WILLIAMS

ILLUSTRATED BY
SARA PALACIOS

EERDMANS BOOKS FOR YOUNG READERS

GRAND RAPIDS, MICHIGAN

Enrique dribbled the ball right past the defense and kicked.

Slam! Into the goal.

"Way to go!" Sam slapped his back. Roger knuckled his head.

The whole team cheered. "We won!"

"We couldn't have done it without you," Sam said. "We're going to the tournament!"

Coach passed out permission slips.

Enrique burst in the door after the game.

"Papá! I scored the winning goal!" He waved the permission slip at his father.

Papá read the paper. He frowned. "I can't sign this."

"But Papá! We're in the tournament."

"And you will have to travel through the checkpoint."

"Papá, I was born here. You told me, I'm a U.S. citizen. You don't have to worry about me."

"I have to think of our family, Enrique. La migra. The border patrol can stop anyone. If they find something on your papers, they could send us back across the border, split us up."

"You're always afraid. Afraid of la migra, the police. Everything!"

"That's enough." Papá crumpled the permission slip and tossed it in the trash.

Enrique ran to his bedroom. "I don't know why you even brought us here to America."

He slammed the door and lay on his bed.

Enrique held back tears when he faced his friends the next day.

"I can't go to the tournament," he said.

"Why not?" Sam asked.

"What do you mean, you can't go?" Roger frowned.

"Because of the checkpoint?" Coach asked.

Enrique nodded, and ran off the field.

"Enrique!" Sam and Roger caught up to him.

"The team needs you. You don't need to be afraid," Sam said.

Roger didn't look at him. "I can't believe you're going to let us all down."

Enrique walked home alone. Why did his father worry so much? *I was born in the U.S. I am an American*, he thought. *My team needs me.*

Enrique made a decision. He was going to the tournament no matter what his dad said. When he got home, he waited for Papá to go to work. Mamá was busy in the kitchen. His sister Rosa wasn't home yet.

Enrique found the crumpled permission slip in the trash. He spread it out and very carefully wrote his father's name in the blank and stuffed the slip into his backpack. He was not going to be afraid like his dad.

The next day, Enrique worried about the permission slip as he walked to school. But Papá would see. Everything would be okay. He would be proud when they won the tournament.

Enrique saw Roger and Sam kicking a ball around the playground. Now he could tell them he was going to the tournament.

Just as he was about to head over to them, someone grabbed his arm. It was Rosa.

"Get in the car." Tía's car.

"La migra," Rosa said. She looked over her shoulder as if the border patrol might be right there. "We're going to Tía's."

Enrique stood still. He had to tell his friends he wasn't going to let them down. He had school today, and practice for the tournament. "I can't leave now."

"You want to put the whole family in danger?" Rosa slammed her door.

"Where are you going?" Sam called from the playground.

Enrique looked down at his feet and got into the car.

At Tía's house the adults sat around the kitchen table.

"La Virgencita de Guadalupe nos protege." Tía looked up at the painting of the Virgin Mary. "This round-up could be just a rumor. Maybe there's no need to fear."

"We'll spend the night anyway," Papá said. "We can't take that chance. Tomás was stopped for a broken taillight. With no documents, look what happened."

Enrique slept with his cousins on the floor. He thought about María, whose father Tomás had been sent back to Mexico. He thought about the permission slip still in his backpack.

Papá did not go to work that night. Enrique found him in the living room with Mamá and Rosa.

"Can't sleep, mijo?"

"Tell me the story of how we came here," Enrique said.

Rosa sighed. "Tell him the whole story, for once. He's ten years old. He should know."

Papá cleared his throat. "Mamá and I came north because we love you and Rosita. We wanted a life where you would be safe, with enough food, no guns shooting."

Enrique knew this part by heart, the best part, about how much his parents loved him and his sister.

"It's not a fairy tale," Rosa said. "I was little then, but I remember."

"Abuelita, tu tío—all our family helped us," Papá continued. "We owe them so much money for the coyote, the man they paid to guide us. The coyote drove us in a van. He knew the best place to cross. But something happened."

Enrique sat up. "What?" This was the part of the
story he had never heard.

"Suddenly lights blinded us. The driver stopped.
Get out. Run. Rápido! Andale!"

Mamá nodded. "We were traveling with others. The Rodríguez baby started to cry."

"Mamá was big with you in her belly," Papá continued. "We ran fast, away from the lights, the cries of the baby, men shouting. We hid behind a huge rock."

"What happened to the Rodríguez family?" Enrique asked.

"We don't know," Rosa answered.

Mamá had tears in her eyes. "That crying baby saved us, took la migra off our trail."

"We walked for two nights with only a little water," Papá added.

Enrique knew the rest. "You found the fence where the coyote cut a hole.
You climbed through and you were in the U.S., so happy you cried."

Later that night Enrique crept out of his sleeping bag, tore up the permission slip, and threw it in the trash.

He skipped practice that week and sat alone at lunch. He was letting his team down and they would never understand.

On Thursday, a bunch of the guys came over to his table. He wanted to hide.

"Enrique," Sam said, "you have to come to the tournament. You're a citizen—you don't have to worry about the checkpoint."

"It's just your dad," Roger said. "He's scared."

Enrique jumped up and pushed back his chair. What did Roger know about fear? Fear of la migra, fear of losing your job, getting sent away. Fear of losing your dad. In his heart he knew the real truth.

"My dad has courage!" he shouted. "He and my mom walked across the desert with hardly any water, and men chasing them. They did it for me and Rosa. They protected us."

Enrique slammed his chair over and left the cafeteria.

On Saturday, the day of the tournament, Enrique stayed in his room. He kicked his soccer ball under his bed. He wondered what his father's courage was worth if he couldn't even go to a soccer tournament.

"Enrique," Mamá called from the kitchen, "there's someone here."

Who? His friends were all at the big game. Maybe he didn't even have any friends.

He opened the door. Coach was there, Sam, the whole team—even Roger.

"What are you doing?" Enrique asked. "What about the game?"

"We voted," Sam explained. "If you can't cross the checkpoint, we won't go either."

"We're a team," Roger added. "And you are right. Your dad is brave."

Papá looked at Enrique. "Tus amigos tienen valor, Enrique. You ask why we came here to this country. This is why we came to the U.S."

Papá put his arm around Enrique.

"There's a father-son game in the park tomorrow," Coach said.

"We'll be there," Papá said. "Our family will be there."

A NOTE FROM THE AUTHOR

Because I have lived for many years outside of my own culture, many of them with my four children, I am drawn to stories from across cultures. While living in the Southwest, I met people who had been stopped more than once at checkpoints in New Mexico and Texas. I wondered how these checkpoints might affect the life of a young person. What would their story be? I talked to an FBI agent who worked along the border. I interviewed a reporter who covered stories on both sides of the Mexico-U.S. border. A story took shape. I drove through checkpoints myself, and in El Paso, Texas, I interviewed children, teachers, and a school social worker who worked both in Mexico and the U.S. I walked along the border where I met children on both sides of the border wall and spoke with border patrol agents. And I read books—piles of books—about border crossings, border towns, and immigrants. Many stories are sad and difficult to read.

I am grateful for those stories and for the time and patience and willingness to share from so many people. Most of them did not know me, many whose names I do not know. Thank you for your honesty and guidance. Lastly, thank you to Sara Palacios for her talent in interpreting this story and bringing it to life.

WHAT IS AN IMMIGRANT?

An immigrant is someone who has left their home to move to a new country. Immigrants come to the United States from all over the world. An undocumented immigrant in the United States is a person who lives there without legal papers like a passport or visa. Some reports say there are more than 10 million people living in the U.S. without permission. But since these people are not here legally, it is difficult to know how many there really are. The number may be much greater. One estimate is that Mexican immigrants make up close to one half of the undocumented population.

Immigrants move to a new country for many different reasons. Most of them are looking for better living conditions for themselves and their families. Some bring their families with them. Many come alone and send money home. They often risk their lives. Crossing the border from Mexico to the United States through the desert or swimming the Rio Grande can be very dangerous. Undocumented immigrants must not only watch out for the border patrol agents but for drug runners and others who want to rob them. Immigrants fleeing their country often hire a "coyote," a person who is paid to smuggle them across the border. Since this is illegal, it is difficult to know who can be trusted. There is the added risk that drug smuggling and other illegal activities could be involved.

In this story, Enrique was born in the U.S. so he is legally a U.S. citizen—but the rest of his family are not citizens. Undocumented immigrants like Papá, Mamá, and Rosa are often fearful that they will be stopped anywhere at any time and asked to show the legal papers they do not have. This could mean being detained or arrested with the threat of being deported back to the country of origin. Families are often split up when this happens, and it may take years for them to find each other again.

WHAT IS A CHECKPOINT?

Inside the United States there are roughly 70 checkpoints operating within up to 100 miles of the border. Most of them are in Arizona, New Mexico, Texas, and California near the border with Mexico. There are similar checkpoints near the Canadian border in states like New York and Maine. The situation is always in flux so the numbers of checkpoints and the laws governing them are often changing. The purpose of the checkpoints is to identify illegal immigrants or others smuggling drugs or participating in other illegal activities.

Anyone traveling in the U.S. can be stopped at these checkpoints and required to prove citizenship. Agents may stop a vehicle at fixed checkpoints for brief questioning of its occupants even if there is no reason to believe that the particular vehicle contains illegal passengers or drugs. Motorists may be referred to a secondary inspection area for more questioning.

ORGANIZATIONS ASSISTING AND ADVOCATING FOR IMMIGRANT FAMILIES

Learn more about these issues and find ways you can get involved by checking out the following organizations.

Al Otro Lado

alotrolado.org

Working in Southern California and Tijuana, Mexico, this organization provides legal services to deportees, refugees, and separated families along the border.

I'm Your Neighbor Books

imyourneighborbooks.org

Based in Portland, Maine, this nonprofit collects and distributes books about immigrants, refugees, and asylum seekers to schools and libraries across the U.S.

Interfaith Immigration Coalition

interfaithimmigration.org

With member organizations from Jewish, Christian, Sikh, and other faith communities, this group advocates for humane and equitable reforms to immigration policy.

Kids In Need of Defense

supportkind.org

Providing legal and social services around the world, KIND assists migrant children in their countries of origin, travel, arrival, and destination.

National Immigration Law Center

nilc.org

In areas including health care, enforcement, and workers' rights, this organization defends and advances the rights of immigrants with low income.

Owl and Panther

owlandpanther.org

Based in Tucson, Arizona, this nonprofit seeks to welcome immigrants through education and experiences with the arts and in nature.

The Young Center for Immigrant Children's Rights

theyoungcenter.org

With offices across the United States, the Young Center serves children in the country's immigration system and advocates for just reform that recognizes children's best interests.

RECOMMENDED READING

Here are some titles that will help add to an understanding and discussion of the themes in this book.

de Anda, Diane. *Mango Moon*. Illus. Sue Cornelison. Park Ridge, Illinois: Albert Whitman, 2019. Picture book.

Bowles, David. *They Call Me Güero: A Border Kid's Poems*. El Paso: Cinco Puntos Press, 2018. Verse novel.

Buitrago, Jairo. *Two White Rabbits*. Illus. Rafael Yockteng. Trans. Elisa Amado. Toronto: Groundwood, 2015. Picture book.

Cisneros, Ernesto. *Efrén Divided*. New York: HarperCollins, 2020. Novel.

Diaz, Alexandra. *Santiago's Road Home*. New York: Simon & Schuster, 2020. Novel.

Henzel, Cynthia Kennedy. *Mexican Immigrants: In Their Shoes*. New York: Momentum, 2017. Juvenile nonfiction.

Laínez, René Colato. *From North to South / Del Norte al Sur*. Illus. Joe Cepeda. New York: Children's Book Press, 2013. Picture book.

Mills, Deborah, and Alfredo Alva. *La Frontera: El Viaje con papá / My Journey with Papa*. Illus. Claudia Navarro. Cambridge, MA: Barefoot Books, 2018. Picture book.

Morales, Yuyi. *Dreamers*. New York: Neal Porter Books, 2018. Picture book.

Perkins, Mitali. *Between Us and Abuela: A Family Story from the Border*. Illus. Sara Palacios. New York: Farrar, Straus and Giroux, 2019. Picture book.

Tonatiuh, Duncan. *Pancho Rabbit and the Coyote: A Migrant's Tale*. New York: Abrams, 2013. Picture book.